HATCHiMALS™

THE SEARCH FOR THE
OOPSY-DAISY

by Mickie Matheis
illustrated by Kellee Riley

PENGUIN YOUNG READERS LICENSES
An Imprint of Penguin Random House

PENGUIN YOUNG READERS LICENSES
An Imprint of Penguin Random House LLC

ISBN 9781524784997   10 9 8 7 6 5 4 3 2 1

The morning sun danced across Ava's face. She squinted, turning to hide her eyes in the pillow. It was too early to get up.

"Wake up!" a voice whispered urgently. It belonged to Ava's younger brother, Oliver. "It's time to go!"

That's when Ava remembered. Today they were going to Hatchtopia to visit the Hatchimals. This was no time for sleeping—it was going to be a magical day!

Ava flung off the covers and flew out of bed.

They had to get to the tree in the backyard as soon as possible.

Hatchtopia was a secret world where friendly, fun-loving creatures called Hatchimals lived. Ava and Oliver had recently hatched their own Hatchimals—Pippi the Penguala and Duke the Draggle—from eggs they'd found in their backyard. Together, they had discovered the world the Hatchimals came from. And a doorway to this world was through the big tree that grew right in their backyard!

Ava and Oliver raced to the tree where Pippi and Duke were waiting. Then the siblings reached out to the tree and tapped . . . ONE . . . TWO . . . THREE . . . on its gnarled trunk.

A small shape appeared at
the base of the tree. The secret door
was opening! It shimmered faintly at first,
but gradually grew brighter.

When the door was
fully formed, Pippi and
Duke tumbled through.

Ava and Oliver quickly followed, shrinking in size
as they entered the wonderful world of Hatchtopia.

"Hello, Hatchtopia!" Ava said joyfully. She looked back at the tree from which they had just emerged. The doorway was already starting to fade. "And hello, Giggling Tree!"

Located in the very center of Hatchtopia, the Giggling Tree spread happiness to anyone who came near it. It also released seeds throughout the land so more trees would grow to provide nests for all the Hatchimals.

The branches of the enormous tree twisted high into the sky. Thousands of tiny lights flickered among its leaves. The Giggling Tree was in full bloom, so its magic was very strong.

Oliver gave the twinkling tree a big hug, and the tree made a funny noise. It was laughing! That made Oliver and Ava laugh, too.

They were so happy to be back in this incredible place. What would they discover on this visit?

"What should we do? Where should we go?" Oliver was so excited that he was practically jumping up and down.

Before Ava could reply, there was a rustling in a nearby Feathered Fern, a delicate purple plant. A Penguala hurried out carrying a notebook and a pencil.

"Good morning," she said, a bit distracted. "My name is Penelope. I'm looking for my best friend, Becky the Burtle. Have you seen her?"

"It's very nice to meet you," Ava said. "I'm sorry, but we haven't seen your friend. We've only just arrived."

"What's a Burtle?" Oliver asked curiously.

"It's a Hatchimal that's part butterfly and part turtle," Penelope said. "Becky and I have been best friends since the day we hatched!"

She explained that she and Becky had planned to meet at the Daisy Schoolhouse in Glittering Garden to work on a project. Penelope had waited, but Becky never arrived and the project was due at the end of the day!

"It's called Explore Hatchtopia. We have a list of things to find and write about," Penelope said. "And now I need to find Becky, too!"

"We can help you," Ava offered. "We'll form teams. Penelope, you lead Oliver and me to search for the things on your list. Pippi and Duke will look for Becky. We'll meet in Glittering Garden before sunset."

"That's so kind," Penelope said gratefully. "Thank you!"

She was especially worried about finding one specific item on the list: the Oopsy-Daisy. This rare flower popped up randomly around Glittering Garden, never growing in the same spot twice.

With a quick wave goodbye, the teams split up and headed off.

"Where to first?" Ava asked.

"Magical Meadow," Penelope replied, looking at her list. "To find a castle."

"Wow! I didn't think there were castles in Hatchtopia," said Oliver.

Penelope paused, looking puzzled. "Neither did I!"

MAGICAL MEADOW—
FIND A CASTLE

As they entered Magical Meadow, they saw a family of Hedgyhens picnicking in a clearing.

"Hello! Excuse us for interrupting your lunch, but can you tell us if there's a castle around here?" Oliver asked. The Hedgyhens shook their heads. They didn't know anything about a castle.

Neither did the Kittycan sunning herself in a eucalyptus tree.

After looking around for a while, the three searchers came across a few Puppits playing tag in the tall grass. "Have you seen a castle?" Penelope asked.

The Puppits stopped running and flopped down on their backs. "Sometimes we do," they said, staring up at the sky. They patted the grass next to them. "Let's look."

Penelope, Ava, and Oliver did as the Puppits asked, and quickly understood what they meant. The clouds over Magical Meadow formed all kinds of fantastic shapes!

"There's a castle right there!" Ava cried, pointing at a puffy cloud. Penelope and Oliver saw it, too—a grand castle with towers and spires and even a drawbridge. "Awesome!" Oliver said.

"Great job!" Penelope said, scribbling in her notebook. They were making good progress, thanks to some helpful Hatchimals.

The trio continued their travels, completing the tasks for the Explore Hatchtopia project one by one.

In Polar Paradise, as Penelope, Ava, and Oliver worked together to build a Burtle out of snow, Oliver discovered an egg.

The boy hugged the egg close while Ava and Penelope gently encouraged it to hatch. The egg cracked, and an adorable Sealark crept out. "Let's call her Sally," Oliver suggested.

Even though he was standing in the coldest place in Hatchtopia, Oliver felt warm inside. Newborn Hatchimals always made him happy.

But Penelope was feeling rather sad. Looking at the snow-Burtle made the Penguala wonder where Becky could be. It wasn't like her to skip out on a school project. She was such a responsible Hatchimal. As the group prepared to leave Polar Paradise, Penelope hoped Pippi and Duke were having better luck in their search for Becky.

Ava, Oliver, and Penelope's next stop was Fabula Forest, a happy, harmonious place with tuneful trees that made their own music. "We need to find Glamberries here," Penelope said.

"Let's ask her," Ava advised, gesturing toward a Deeraloo standing near a Pink Maple tree. But the Deeraloo said she didn't eat berries. She suggested checking with the Chipadees chasing each other along the branches of a nearby Orchid Pine tree.

The Chipadees didn't know where to find Glamberries, either. "Ask the Raspoons!" they chattered, pointing to a large Lavender Oak tree. "They'll know where the Glamberries are hiding. They're hatch-and-seek experts!"

A pair of Raspoons were playing inside a hole in the trunk of the gigantic tree. Penelope asked if they knew where to find Glamberries.

"Of course! That's easy. Follow us!" the Raspoons replied, running along a forest path until they stopped in front of some twisted, twinkling vines.

"But those are vines," Oliver told them.
The Raspoons giggled. "Just wait." They
scampered all the way to the top of the
plants. "Ready?"
They grabbed on to the vines and started
to slide down. As they did, the twisted vines
straightened, revealing clusters of tiny, shiny
berries hidden inside!

Penelope, Ava, and Oliver reached inside and plucked off a few Glamberries to taste. They were delicious—both sweet and tart at the same time.

Penelope wrote about the experience in her notebook and thanked the Raspoons. Then she and the siblings headed out of Fabula Forest.

They joined a Girreo for a leisurely cruise around Lilac Lake. Oliver laughed when his hands turned light purple after using them to paddle.

They hiked up a steep, glistening mountain in Crystal Canyon with a pair of Owlicorn guides, to tour a cave covered in sparkling rainbow crystals.

They collected shining shells from Breezy Beach, removing their shoes to let the soft sand squish pleasantly between their toes. Penelope wished Becky were there to join in the fun.

Although Penelope missed Becky, she was happy to have made two new friends in Ava and Oliver. The sister and brother seemed to be having a lot of fun. But there was only one more item on the list to find—the Oopsy-Daisy.

Penelope showed Ava and Oliver a picture of the white flower. "But not much is known about it, other than it grows somewhere in Glittering Garden," she explained. "And it's usually found by accident."

The Oopsy-Daisy is a very rare flower that grows in Glittering Garden.

When the trio arrived at Glittering Garden, Pippi and Duke were already there, having found no sign of Becky. Together, they all began to search.

Penelope got butter all over her wings while looking through a bunch of Buttercups.

Ava and Pippi had to shield their eyes from the bright light as they pushed through a patch of Shining Sunflowers.

Oliver and Duke kept getting kissed by the playful Eightlips as they leaned down to look among them. "Stop!" Oliver laughed, wiping his cheeks.

But there was no sign of the Oopsy-Daisy.

"Where could it be? We've searched every inch of this garden!" Penelope said. "It's like it's invisible."

Oliver kicked a stick in disappointment. He had really wanted to help Penelope finish her project and meet Becky the Burtle. Now it looked like neither of those things would happen!

"Let's stop and think," Ava suggested. They needed to hatch a new plan for finding the Oopsy-Daisy.

Suddenly, they heard a strange noise. It seemed to be coming from a colorful rock bed in the farthest corner of Glittering Garden.

Zzzzzzzzz.

They all looked at one another. What in the world could *that* be?

Everyone hurried over to the rock bed and climbed up the sides. Penelope peered down and gasped. A giant white flower was snugly tucked inside! She reached down and carefully peeled back a few petals. Peacefully snoozing inside the oversize daisy was Becky, the missing Burtle.

"Becky!" Penelope exclaimed. "There you are!"

The startled Burtle quickly sat up. She yawned and stretched and looked around at the faces staring at her. "Oh, good morning, Penelope," Becky said. "Is it time to start our project already? And who are your friends?"

Penelope told Becky that the day was nearly done—and so was their project. She explained that Ava and Oliver had helped her with it while Pippi and Duke looked for Becky.

"Oh dear," the Burtle said, terribly upset that she had let her friend down. She said she had arrived at school very early that morning to do some research for their project. By the time she finished looking at maps, taking notes, and plotting their route through Hatchtopia, she was too tired to keep her eyes open.

"I thought I'd take a nap," Becky said. She had decided to rest in the cool quiet of the colorful rock bed. "I found this super-cozy flower. But now I've overslept and ruined everything!" The Burtle burst into tears.

"No you didn't, Becky. This is the Oopsy-Daisy!" Penelope said excitedly. She pulled out her notebook and flipped to the page with the flower. Ava and Oliver huddled over her to compare the picture with the actual flower. It matched!

"The Oopsy-Daisy was the last thing we needed for our report—and *you* found it!" Penelope said.

"I did? I mean, wow!" Becky said, now blushing with happiness.

"You saved the day!" Ava said.

"You finished our report!" added Penelope.

"And I got to meet a Burtle—*and* help hatch a Sealark!" Oliver cheered, giving Duke a hatch-five.

Penelope laughed and gave Becky a big hug before turning to Ava, Oliver, Pippi, and Duke. "Thank you so much for helping me," she said sincerely. "This has been an absolutely magical day!"

"It's *always* a magical day when you spend it with friends," Ava said. She and Oliver waved goodbye to their new Hatchimal pals—until the next time!